The Sun Ic

In " The Sun Loves Me," Mansa discovers how the sun plays a pivotal role in the uniqueness of his dark skin and nappy hair, and how his African ancestors, the original inhabitants of this earth whom have these same beautiful features as him, play a major role in the creation and evolution of this planet.

Written by
Dynast Amir
Illustrated by
Yashar Clemons

Foreword

Be it ridicule, curiosity, bigotry, ignorance or pride, the day will come where our children will know that they are unique in physical features from others. We as parents, as a people, have the power and the duty to fortify the images of who they are, what they are, and who they will be, so that when the day of ridicule, curiosity, bigotry or ignorance presents itself, they are filled with pride as they proclaim that their beauty and intelligence are gifts. That they come from the people that have been kissed by the one thing all men can see with their eyes and feel on their skin, The thing that sustains all life on planet earth: the SUN.

--Khadijah Hassan

"Walk in the Light of the sun, as if all can see you at all times. Bathe in the light of the sun as if it can, as it does, heal all things. Take each step in its warmth as if the sun is your true loving parent, and think of it as the source of all life, as we all know it is. For without the sun there would be no life, as we know it. This we all know."

-- Tehuti

There was a boy named Mansa,
Who's skin was cocoa brown.
His hair was kinky and curly,
He wore a high top fade around
town.

He kicked soccer balls.
Shot basketball like the other kids
do.
He always made straight A's,
For this was nothing new.

One day, Peter and John asked
Mansa on the bus,
"Why is your skin and hair different
from us?"

"Why is your skin and hair different from us?"
Peter asked,"Why is your skin the color of mud like the wet ground?"
"You look like you are covered in soil from foot to brow."

John asked, "Is your hair frizzy or is it just me?"

"How did your hair become so thick?"

"Is that what they call nappy?"

Mansa could not answer and was so ashamed.
When he got off the bus he ran home to ask his parents, hoping they could explain.

Almost in tears Mansa asked his parents, " Mom and Dad, why does my skin look like I have been covered with soil from foot to brow?"

"Why is my hair called nappy for all
to question how?"
Mansa's mom hugged him and said
"Son, God formed man from dust
from the ground."
'That is why your skin is beautiful
and deep brown."
"And your hair is your connection to
the sun and it links us to the
ancestral ones."
"Ancestors?" asked Mansa.
"Who are the ancestors?"

"Mansa, our ancestors are the original people of the sun."

"They came first to this earth before anyone."

"Our dark skin and kinky hair can be compared to none."

"This is what makes you, me and the ancestors united as one."

"We are forever linked to the ancestors through our D.N.A."

"They are whom we talk to when we pray."

"We are divinely unique as you can see."

"For no one on this earth has hair and skin like you and me."

"Now take this book and browse through the pages of our history,
and marvel at the facts that you will read and see."

Mansa opened up the book and
began to read about the greatness of
Black History.
"Wow!!!" Mansa exclaimed,
"Knowledge is gold."
"These are the greatest stories ever
told."

"The great pyramids were built by my ancestors whom came before me."

"They all had kinky hair and black skin just like me!"

"Abubakari, before Columbus, crossed the great sea."
"The world's richest man of all time, Mansa Musa, had dark skin and kinky hair just like me!"
"That's awesome!!!" Mansa shouted joyfully, " I was named after Mansa Musa.""I knew that he was rich, but I didn't know that he was named the richest man in history."

"Martin, Malcolm, and Nefertiti,..........
Marcus Garvey and Maya Angelou
all look like me!"

"Moses was an African whom parted the Red Sea."
"Even Jesus of Galilee had skin of bronze and hair like wool just like me!"

The next day when Mansa went out to play.
He was anxious to tell Peter and John what he learned yesterday.

"After reading through the pages of
my black history,
"I am proud of my skin and my hair
for my features are unique you see."

"My ancestors are the original people of the sun."
"Their accomplishments are second to none."
"They had dark skin and kinky hair just like me."
"So, wherever life's journey leads me to be."
"There is one thing for certain, **THE SUN LOVES ME**."

THE END

The sun loves me

Author's Note

I give thanks to the ancestors, whom are the original people of the sun, for utilizing me as a channel to produce this work. Hopefully this book could be used as a tool to aid in the restoration of our most ancient African history throughout black communities across the globe. As a youth, I always inquired on the origins of African peoples and when I could not find the answers in standardized textbooks, I took the initiative to uncover the facts myself. Some of these facts I share with you throughout these pages. "The Sun Loves Me" is a resource for kids to discover their roots and a tool to help build a strong foundation in the shaping of a child's true identity. Their identity is directly connected to a lineage of the first people whom dwelled and set the foundation for all others on this planet called earth. Kids will begin to internalize the maxim "Know Thy Self" and in knowing thy self, they will know all others, and in knowing all others they will be provided with the mastery to command the universe.

-- Dynast Amir

Special thanks to my Mom, Dad, Ancestors, Ramone, Khadijah for the foreword, Yashar for the illustrations and Natalia for the finishing touches

Dynast Amir was born in Sacramento, CA. He found his passion for writing through journaling everyday. Dynast has been consistently traveling to Africa since 2011, and plans on relocating to Nigeria and Sierra Leone soon. His ambition in life is to purchase lands for afflicted souls and to possess more gold than Mansa Musa. Dynast currently serves as the Omo Oba "Prince" of Ororuwo, Nigeria and invites everyone to come and visit the Kingdom of Ororuwo one day.

Yashar Clemons is a native of Los Angeles, CA. Just recently graduating from Chico State University in Chico, California, he is in the process of debuting his own comic book series. Yashar's ambition is to be a professional animator and to uplift souls through art. In accomplishing this, he believes that he will experience true happiness. "I want to make a living doing what I love to do best."

The sun loves me

Manufactured in the United States of America

ISBN: 978-1-7346383-0-1

Publisher/Author contact: info@noirisme.com

For information regarding discounts or bulk purchases, please visit our

website or email info@noirisme.com

Made in the USA
San Bernardino, CA
25 May 2020